.The Carpenter's Carpet

.

The Carpenter's Carpet

·

Ian D. K. Kelly

Old stories in new words

The Carpenter's Carpet

First published 2007 Agrintha Books Ltd, Exeter UK

agrinthabooks@blueyonder.co.uk

This edition 2021 IDKK Publications, Chobham, GU24 8QP

idkk@idkk.com

ISBN 978-1-9997226-3-0

Contents

Birthday Party   1

The Woodcutter's Horse   3

A Pot of Butter   6

Noah   8

Yellow Coat   11

Swimming   13

Sparrows   15

The Carpenter's Carpet   17

Dreamer's Well   19

The Old Man and the Goat   23

Diamond Cut Diamond   25

Sweet Water   31

The Kurd's Camel   33

Think Ahead   35

For Miranda
with a promise of more

The Carpenter's Carpet

.Birthday Party

ONCE UPON A TIME there was a little boy who was a special little boy. He lived in a far-away land called Vrindavan. The little boy's name was Krishna, and unlike you and me his skin was coloured blue — so blue it was almost black. Fancy that! A little dark blue baby chuckling and gurgling in his cradle!

It was Krishna's first birthday, and his mother Yashoda had arranged for a big party to which everyone in the village was invited. She rushed this way and that — dusting the furniture, polishing the pans, arranging the flowers, cooking the rice, mixing the yoghurt — and she was so busy that Yashoda quite forgot to give Krishna his lunch. Poor Krishna! He was hungry! And by the time the guests arrived for the party, he started to cry. But the visitors made so much noise laughing and talking and singing, that Yashoda couldn't hear her little son Krishna crying.

Now *your* Mummy and Daddy don't keep cows in their front room, do they? But Krishna's Mummy and Daddy sometimes did have cows in their house — it was their job to look after cattle, the cows and the bulls. *Your* Mummy puts the dishes on the sideboard or on the table, but Yashoda put all the birthday presents that Krishna was getting on an ox-cart — that is a trailer big enough for two cows to pull it! Krishna's cradle was near this ox-cart so that he could see all the lovely presents he was being given — but Krishna wasn't thinking about presents — he was still hungry. He cried, and kicked his feet around. One of his little feet hit the wheel of the ox-cart; and, do you know, he

1

kicked it *so* hard that the wheel actually broke. All the presents and pots and pans and bowls of fruit and yoghurt and rice and nuts that Yashoda had put on the ox-cart fell to the floor with a CRASH! I *told* you Krishna was a special little boy.

The crash brought everybody running to Krishna, and when Yashoda saw her baby was crying, she remembered that she had not given him his lunch, so she gave him some nice warm milk straight away. Little Krishna wasn't hungry any more — and everybody at the party wondered why it was that the ox-cart had collapsed. Nobody believed the little children who told how they had seen the baby Krishna kick the wheel: all the grown-ups thought Krishna was too tiny to be so strong.

But Krishna was happy again, and everybody sang birthday songs.

The Carpenter's Carpet

.The Woodcutter's Horse

ONCE UPON A TIME — not so very long ago — there was a rich kingdom. The people living there knew all about growing plants, building beautiful houses, making wonderful machines, painting elegant pictures, and singing sweet music.

One day Mumkin, the King, decided to hold a competition — a contest — to find who in the kingdom could make the best invention. Two men decided to enter for the competition — an ironsmith, and a woodworker. The smith took lots of metal and locked himself away behind high walls with many clever people to work hard on his invention. The Woodworker took his simple tools, and went into a forest to think, alone, and began to work on his.

Eventually both of them were ready, and the King asked to see the new inventions. The smith produced a big metal fish which, he said, could swim on and under the water, and carry heavy weights across land. Everyone was astonished at the things the fish could do, and were yet more amazed when the smith showed them that the fish could even fly slowly through the air. The King was delighted and gave lots of presents to the smith for his wonderful fish. King Mumkin asked his first son Hoshyar to work with the smith and make more of these wonderful metal fish, so that everyone could have one.

Then the carpenter brought his invention forward. It was a simple wooden horse, nicely carved and painted.
"It looks like a toy," said the King: "what is it for?"
"Your Majesty," stammered the woodcarver, "it is a magic

3

horse. You have to *tell* the fish what to do, but this horse knows the desires of its rider, and takes him where he wishes to go, without being asked."

"Hmm," muttered the King, "it doesn't sound as useful as the metal fish. I don't think it is worth any money. Give it to my second son, Tambal: he is always dreaming about nonsense — he will like the toy."

So the horse was given to Tambal, and the woodcutter went sadly away, because no-one said they liked his invention.

Tambal took the horse to his room and looked at it carefully. He found the horse had little knobs on it which you could twist. He also found that if he sat on the wooden horse and twisted the knobs, the horse rose in to the air and flew very fast to wherever he was thinking of — Tambal didn't have to *tell* it where. Tambal liked the horse, and thought it was much better than his brother's fish.

One day Tambal sat on the back of the horse and thought: "I wish I could find my heart's desire: whatever it is that I *really* want most, that would make me happy", and he twisted the knobs on the neck of the little wooden horse. Quicker than you can blink your eye the horse flew far, far away to another kingdom, where a beautiful Princess lived in a magic floating palace — a castle that floated on air. Because his little wooden horse was able to fly so quickly, Tambal was able to get to the palace of Princess Durri-Karima. There he met the lovely Princess, and they fell in love.

Now it was a bad man, a naughty man, who had put the Princess in this palace from which she could not escape, and he tried to steal Tambal's wonderful horse. But the Princess and Tambal were too quick for him, and sitting on the little wooden horse they twiddled the knobs and wished themselves back in Tambal's kingdom.

King Mumkin was very surprised to see his son come back with the beautiful Princess, whom even Hoshyar agreed was charming. And when Tambal married the lovely Durri-Karima everyone who saw her agreed that perhaps, after all, the wooden horse had brought more wonderful things to the land than the metal fish.

I think the woodcutter got his reward after all.

The Carpenter's Carpet

.A Pot of Butter

ONE DAY Krishna had been a very naughty boy. His mother, Yashoda, was feeding him when the milk started boiling over on the stove. So quickly Yashoda put him down and rushed to take the milk off — she didn't want it to boil over and burn on the heat. This did not please the baby Krishna, who had been enjoying his meal. So when his mother went away, Krishna very naughtily broke his mother's pot of butter, stole some butter from it, and ran away to eat it in a corner.

When Yashoda came back and saw her pot of butter broken and Krishna gone, she knew that Krishna had broken it and was cross with him. She picked up her big flat butter-pat, and went to look for her little son: she was going to give him a big smack! She looked for him everywhere — in the kitchen, in the bedrooms, and in the cow-byre where the cows slept. At last Yashoda found Krishna behind the shed, sitting on a great big upturned wooden bowl, sharing the butter he had stolen with the monkeys!

Krishna saw his mother approaching, and knew that she would be cross. He saw the big flat butter-pat in her hand, and he did not want a big smack – so Krishna ran away again. Yashoda ran after him, and they chased round and round the house, until she caught him. Krishna began to cry, and although Krishna had been very naughty, Yashoda loved Krishna so much that she did not want him to be too upset. She put down her butter-pat, and decided that instead of giving Krishna the smack he deserved, she would leave him tied to the wooden bowl — the one she had found him sitting on. A few hours there would be enough punishment.

So Yashoda held the crying Krishna firmly by the hand and dragged him along while she went to fetch a rope. When she had found one she took it and Krishna back to the big wooden bowl and tried to bind him to it. But the rope was two inches too short.

Yashoda took Krishna and the rope and went back in to the house to get another length of rope. When she found one she took Krishna and the two pieces of rope back to the big wooden bowl, knotted the two pieces of rope together, and again started to tie Krishna up.

But the rope was *still* two inches too short!

Yashoda was puzzled, but she took Krishna and the two pieces of rope and went to look for some more rope. Krishna was still crying, because he *had* been a very naughty boy, and he didn't want to be punished. But Yashoda found a third length of rope and tied it to the end of the other two, and took Krishna and the ropes back to the big wooden bowl. But, do you know, the three ropes together were *still* two inches too short.

Yashoda was very puzzled indeed, and looked at the ropes and then at Krishna. Krishna stopped crying and smiled at his mother, then Krishna laughed and decided to stop playing his special tricks on his mother — and suddenly the first piece of rope was long enough to go round the baby Krishna and the big wooden bowl not just once, not just twice, but three times.

And there his Mummy left him till tea-time — well, he *had* been a naughty boy, hadn't he?

7

The Carpenter's Carpet

.Noah

THERE WAS A MAN called Noah, and Noah was a good man even when most other men were bad. He had three sons whose names were Ham, Shem and Japheth, and Noah was very careful to teach them to say their prayers and to be polite, obedient and helpful.

God looked at the way all the other men on earth were behaving, and decided they were like wicked children and had to be punished. But Noah had been a good man, so God didn't want to punish him too. So God said to Noah "build a boat" and although Noah was very puzzled as to *why* he should build a boat, he did build it — just the way that God told him to: Noah was very obedient to God.

And then God said to Noah "take some of every sort of animal and bird into your boat", and Noah did. There were two giraffes and two pigs, two hamsters, two rabbits, and two baboons. There was a lady elephant and a gentleman elephant; a lady hippopotamus and a gentleman hippopotamus; a boy and girl rhinoceros, seven camels, seven sheep, seven cows, and lots of others. It must have been a very big boat, mustn't it?

When they were all aboard they pulled up the gangplank, and Noah carefully shut the door. Ham made sure the window was sealed. Shem told the crocodile not to talk so loudly to the water-dragon, and Japheth stopped the parrots from squabbling with the penguins. And they waited.

It started to rain. Firstly a little light rain just making the air wet, then little drips which showed on the ground, then enough to make the ground muddy, then sploshy puddles going plop-plop-plop. And the puddles got bigger and met each other, and everybody's shoes got wet. And it went on raining: the water got deeper and everyone's knees got wet. It went on raining, and people's furniture floated away. All the bad men who were not in Noah's boat began to feel very uncomfortable, and wished they hadn't been so naughty. But it was too late now — it kept on raining. Noah's boat began to float and all the bad men had to swim.

And it rained for forty days and forty nights – that's a day and a night for each one of your fingers, and a day and a night for each one of Mummy's fingers, and a day and a night for each one of Daddy's fingers, *and* a day and a night for each one of your toes. All the bad men were washed away in so much water, leaving only Captain Noah and his floating zoo.

Everywhere was covered with water for a long time — nearly half a year — even the tops of the hills. But gradually the water dried up, and Noah's boat — the Ark — touched the ground at the top of a mountain called Ararat. Noah waited for the ground to dry, and then opened the window very carefully. He asked one of the ravens to go out and look around — but that black and lovely bird, the raven, could not find anywhere to rest outside of the Ark — it was still too wet. So Noah waited a bit longer.

Then he asked one of the doves to fly out, but it couldn't find anywhere to rest outside of the Ark, so it came back too. And Noah and Ham and Shem and Japheth and their wives waited a bit longer. They sent the dove out again, and that evening the gentle bird with soft white feathers came fluttering back with a little twig of green olive-leaves in its

9

bill, so they knew the tops of the olive-trees at least were out of the water.

All the animals and birds inside the Ark were very excited — I think they must have been very tired of being in the boat for so long, don't you? At last they sent the dove out again — and it didn't come back, so everyone in the Ark knew that the dove had found dry land. Noah opened the door carefully and looked around. Yes, the ground was quite dry. Noah let all the birds and animals out of the Ark: Ham opened the window and shooed out the robins and the chickens, the blackbirds and the owls. His wife picked up the mice and the moles, the hamsters and the guinea-pigs and carried them out: they were too small to walk down the gangplank by themselves. Shem put the monkeys and gorillas, mandrills and baboons on the back of one elephant, and sat with his wife on the back of the other. Japheth herded off the cows and camels, sheep and goats helped by his wife — and the two sheep-dogs. And last of all Noah and his wife with the alligators and horses and donkeys and lions left the Ark.

They all gathered to give a big "thank you" to God for saving them from punishment, just like Mummy and Daddy say "thank you" to God at meal-times. God was pleased, and promised Noah that never again would He punish men like that. He made the rainbow and put it in the sky to remind men of His promise that, as long as the earth continues, seed-sowing and harvest, cold and heat, summer and winter, and day and night will never cease.

We still see rainbows to remind us today.

.*Yellow Coat*

WHEN I WAS AN INFANT CHILD in the Palace of my
Father, and resting in the wealth and luxury of those that
care for me, my parents made for me a great treasure from
the jewels of that land. And they made this treasure light
enough for me to carry alone. But they took from me the
beautiful coat which they had made: the yellow coat
spangled with gold and jewels — with white pearls, green
emeralds, red rubies, the collar encrusted with pale blue
turquoise and glittering diamonds. They took from me the
coat made to fit me. They made a bargain with me, and told
me not to forget it. They said "If you go down to Egypt and
bring back the one great pearl round which the serpent is
coiled, then you shall have back again your lovely yellow
coat, and be like your brother with us."

So I went down to Egypt with two guides to show me the
way, which was easy; and when I got there they left me. I
went straight away to the home of the snake and stood by
the entrance of his deep cave, waiting for him to sleep, to
take my pearl.

I was a stranger in that strange land, and I took to wearing
the clothes of the Egyptians to be less noticeable, but I was
deceived and tasted their food too. Then I forgot I was my
Father's son, and I forgot the pearl for which I was sent, and
I slept.

But my forefathers learned of my state and sent me a letter
which said "From your Father the King, and your Mother
that rules the East, and your brother with us, To our son

11

The Carpenter's Carpet

that is in Egypt, Peace and Greetings. Rise up and awake out of sleep and listen to this letter. Remember that you are the son of a King, not sent to be enslaved in Egypt, but to fetch the great pearl. Remember the wonderful coat that you should wear to be like your brother. Awake, remember, and return to us."

And I received the letter and I remembered that I was a son of a King, and longed to be free again. I remembered for what I had come, and I overcame the serpent, snatching up the pearl. I turned for home and took off the filthy clothes of the serpent's land, and guided by the letter, made my way home again.

And suddenly I saw once more that beautiful yellow coat: Oh! I had forgotten its wonderful brightness, for I was still a child and very young when I had left it in the Palace of my Father. But the coat had grown with me, and was like me, and was the coat of a King. And I took it in knowledge and love, dressed and made beautiful in the exquisiteness of its colours.

Thus royally robed I came to my Father's palace and sat down with my Mother and Brother, where all servants sing sweetly before the King.

.Swimming

IN VRINDAVAN, where Krishna lived, there was no need to have a bathroom in the house, for the beautiful river Yumna flowed close by. When people wanted to wash they went down to the river bank, in a spot sheltered by trees and reeds, and washed in the clear cold waters which ran swiftly by.

One morning several of the young girls of the area gathered on the banks of the Yumna, chattering, laughing and playing in the early morning sunshine which was not yet too hot. These were the girls that looked after the cows, and they were called 'gopis' because of that, for 'go' means 'cow' in their language. They all intended to have a bathe together: with a bath as big as a river you don't have to get in one at a time.

They first looked around carefully to make sure that no men or boys were about before unwinding their beautiful long saris, and leaving them lying on the ground away from the water, airing in the sun. And completely naked, they held hands in a line by the edge of the river, ran towards the water — jumped — and … SPLASH!!! Oooh! The water was cold; and they laughed and chattered while they washed.

When they had bathed enough they looked to see where they had left their clothes to go and fetch them, but — horrors! they were gone. The girls stood in the water and cried out in dismay "Where are our clothes? Who can have taken them? Whatever shall we do?"

13

The Carpenter's Carpet

"O Gopis," called a voice they all knew, "do you want your saris back?"

"Krishna!" exclaimed the girls, "you naughty boy! Whatever are you up to now? Of course we want our clothes back!"

Krishna laughed that lovely musical laugh of his, and peeped his head out from between the branches of the tree he had climbed. "Well," he said, "you must come and get them — I have them all up here in the tree."

"But Krishna," the gopis protested, "how can we? We are naked."

Krishna laughed all the louder. "You can hardly *not* come: I do not think you would want to go to your homes to get other clothes dressed as you are — or rather, **un**dressed as you are! So come up one at a time and I will let you have them back."

The girls were getting quite cold by now and they agreed there was nothing else to do. So they queued up, and one at a time they came to the foot of Krishna's tree, where he made them salute him with the palms of their hands together at their foreheads, like this … before he dropped each one her sari, and blew her a kiss. And, you know, even though he *had* been a rather naughty boy, the gopis didn't *really* mind: they were all so fond of Krishna that that one blown kiss made it all worthwhile.

.Sparrows

THERE ARE LOTS OF STORIES ABOUT JESUS, but maybe you've not heard this one before. It's about when He was a little boy.

It had just stopped raining, and the sun had started to shine. All the children went outdoors to play. It was the Sabbath day, when you were not allowed to do any work at all, even when you were playing. You were not allowed to make things, you were not allowed to write, you were not allowed to carry things, and you were not allowed to touch money. If you did any of these things — and quite a few other things — it was called "breaking the Sabbath," and the grown-ups said that was very naughty. So the children could not carry any toys with them, but they were running and singing and laughing together.

After a while they all sat down together to get their breath back and to chat to each other. They sat around Jesus, because they all loved Him.

All except one. One little boy — the oldest of them — his name was Judas — was a nasty little boy, and he wanted to get Jesus in to trouble. "Let's see what we can make with this mud," said Judas to Jesus, "you go first."

Jesus smiled, and even though He knew it was against the rules to squeeze the mud and to make things on the Sabbath day, He took some of the mud and made models of little birds. He lined the birds up at the edge of a puddle left over from the rain. The younger children thought the birds were wonderful, but did not dare to make anything themselves.

15

The Carpenter's Carpet

And Judas did not pick up any mud to make a model, either — instead he shouted out loudly "Daddy! Mummy! Come quickly! Look! Jesus is breaking the Sabbath!"

Jesus looked down at the model birds and clapped His hands. And, do you know, before the grown-ups came running up, the children saw the mud birds turn in to real sparrows and fly away.

When the grown-ups arrived, the children all told them how Jesus had made birds that flew away, which the adults thought was just a story. And Judas was severely told off by his Mummy and Daddy for telling lies. Judas was very upset — but he had been naughty, hadn't he?

I wonder whether Judas ever came to love Jesus?

.The Carpenter's Carpet

THERE WAS — ONCE UPON A TIME — A CARPENTER. He made many things — some big things, some small things, and some which were in between. The big things were very big — much bigger than me; the small things were very small — much smaller than littlest lady-bug you have ever seen, and the things that were in between … well, they were about as big as you. And everything was just the right size, and beautifully made.

The Carpenter had a Carpet. It was a beautiful carpet, a rug. It was just as long as the distance between your head and your toes. And it didn't matter if you were a big tall grown up or you were a little tiny baby — the carpet always stretched exactly from your head to your toes when you lay down on it. It was a magic carpet, and the Carpenter looked after it very carefully.

What kind of magic could the carpet do? If you sat on the carpet you were granted one wish — just one. The carpet would give you exactly what you wished for. You could wish for a beautiful palace surrounded by gorgeous gardens and — ping! — that's what you would receive. But you couldn't then ask for a chocolate milkshake, or a rocking horse or a colouring book. Or you could ask for an ice-cream and — ping! — there would be the most delicious ice-cream that you had ever tasted. But then you couldn't ask for a pair of football boots or a china doll. You had just one wish.

17

The Carpenter's Carpet

One day, a thoughtless man sat down on the carpet and said "I wish for a carpet that looks exactly like this one, but that gives you the *opposite* of what you ask for." What a silly wish! But — ping! There suddenly appeared another carpet. It was a magic carpet as well. The two carpets were the same colours, and the same size, and the same design. As the silly man was comparing the carpets he got confused as to which was which, and he angrily threw them both down on the floor and stamped away.

When the next person came to make his wish he did not know which was the good carpet and which was the bad carpet. He did not know which carpet would grant his wish, and which would give him the opposite of his wish. "Don't worry," said the Carpenter, "you can still make one good wish and get what you really want, if you think carefully."

Now how could he do that, I wonder? Do you know how?

The Carpenter's Carpet

.Dreamer's Well

ONCE — THOUGH I CANNOT TELL YOU WHEN — there was a man who dreamed rather than work — in fact, they called him "Dreamer". So Dreamer had very little money and his wife was always scolding him. "We are starving," she would say, "go and do some work so that we can get some food."

So one day, Dreamer got up and made ready for a journey to find work. He set out and started walking through the nearby forest towards the king's city. Evening came, and he needed water to drink. He looked around and found a well that was overgrown with grass. He pulled the grass away and looked down to see whether there was any water in the well. But instead of water, at the bottom of the well there was a tiger, a monkey, a snake and a man.

The tiger roared up at Dreamer: "Oh honourable man, please lower the rope and pull me out of this well, so that I can go back and live with my friends and family. It would be an act of virtue."

But Dreamer was frightened: "The very sound of your voice makes me shiver with fear — I am scared to help you." The tiger said: "I swear that I will not harm you." So Dreamer pulled the tiger out of the well.

Then the monkey called out: "Oh honourable man, please pull me too out of this well. I swear that only good will come of it."
So Dreamer pulled the monkey out of the well.

19

The Carpenter's Carpet

Then the snake called out: "Oh honourable man, me too!"
But Dreamer said "Some snakes are even more dangerous
than tigers. I am scared to help you."
And the snake said: "We do not bite unless we must. I
swear that I will not harm you."
So Dreamer pulled the snake out of the well.

The three animals thanked Dreamer, and then each one said:
"The man that is in the well — do not pull him out — do
not help him — do not trust him."
The tiger said: "Do you see the mountain there? The cave
where I live is in a wooded valley on the North side. Do
come and visit me and my family there." And the tiger
bounded off.
The monkey said: "I live close to the tiger's cave, by a
waterfall. Do come and visit me there." And the monkey
swung off through the trees.
The snake said: "In any emergency, remember I am your
friend." And the snake smoothly slid away.

The man in the well shouted: "Pull me out too! Pull me out
too!"
Dreamer thought: "He is just a man — surely I should be
merciful to him too?" and so Dreamer pulled the man out of
the well.
The man said "I am a goldsmith and I live in the king's city.
If you have any gold to be worked you must bring it to me."
And the man started off for his home.

Dreamer continued his wanderings, but found no work to
do, he received no money and he was hungry. Dreamer
remembered the monkey and decided to call on the monkey
as he passed the mountain. The monkey, and the monkey's
family, welcomed Dreamer greatly. They saw that he was

hungry and brought him much sweet fruit — it was
delicious and made Dreamer feel much better.

"Please show me where the tiger lives," said Dreamer, and
the monkey took him to the tiger's cave.
The tiger welcomed Dreamer and gave him a beautiful gold
necklace and fine gold bracelets and other ornaments — all
of gold. "Where did you get these?" asked Dreamer.
"A prince was thrown off his horse near here," said the
tiger, "and I took these ornaments off him and kept them
here. Please take them for yourself."
Dreamer thanked him, and remembered the man he had
pulled from the well. "Perhaps he can sell this gold for me,"
he thought, "and then I will have money to give my wife."

Dreamer went to the goldsmith's house, where he was made
very welcome, comfortably seated and given food and drink.
"What may I do for you, sir?" asked the goldsmith.
"I have brought you some gold,' said Dreamer, "please sell it
for me." And Dreamer handed the gold ornaments to the
goldsmith.
The goldsmith was astonished — he could see that these
were ornaments that he had made for the prince of that
region. "Please make yourself and wait here, while I find
out how much this gold is worth."

The goldsmith went immediately to the king's court, and
showed the gold to the king. "Where did you get this?"
demanded the king.
"In my house there is a man — he brought it to me."
"This man must have killed my son," thought the king: "he
will learn what that costs!" He ordered: "The man in the
goldsmith's house — bring him to me in chains!" and

21

immediately a group of soldiers rushed off to arrest Dreamer.

When Dreamer was bound in chains and thrown in to prison he did not know what to do. He remembered the snake he had pulled from the well — and immediately the snake was there. "What can I do for you?" asked the snake. "Get me free!" said Dreamer.

The snake thought for a moment, then said "I shall bite the king's wife, and make sure that she does not recover until you have touched her with your hand. Then they will let you go free."

The snake slid off, and bit the queen. The queen collapsed and there was uproar and distress in the palace. All the wise men and conjurers and doctors and alchemists were called to remove the poison from the queen but none of them succeeded. A loud announcement was made calling all who could help to come and help. Then Dreamer said to the prison guards "I can cure her." When he had said this they took the chains off him, and brought him to the king.

The king glared at him: "Cure her, and you will be free. If you do not cure her you will be horribly punished." Dreamer reached out his hand and touched the queen, and immediately she was well again. Everyone — especially the king — was astonished and happy that the poison had left the queen. "But tell me," said the king, "how did you come by this gold, which was the gold of my son, the prince?" Dreamer told him the full story, from beginning to end, and the king understood. "I judged you too soon," said the king, "before I knew all facts." And the king gave Dreamer ample money to keep Dreamer — and his wife — happy for many years.

.*The Old Man and the Goat*

"I WOULD LIKE A GOAT," said the old man, "it will give me milk and warm wool, and it can be my pet too." So the old man looked under his mattress, where he kept his money, and took out his last gold coin. He walked through the woods to the next village where he bought a fine goat at the market, picked the goat up and put it on his shoulders to walk home.

There were in the woods three rogues who whispered together about how they could get the goat. "Let us trick him," they said, and if he gives the goat to us it will not be stealing.

The first rogue approached the old man. "Good evening, sir," said the first rogue. "Why are you carrying that dog on your shoulders?"
"Don't be silly," said the old man, "it's not a dog I'm carrying, it's a goat."
"Do not be angry," said the first rogue, "but be careful. These woods are haunted."

When the old man had carried the goat a little further he was met by the second rogue. "Good evening, sir," said the second rogue. "Why are you carrying that young cow on your shoulders?"
"Preposterous man!" exclaimed the old man, "it is not a cow, it is a goat I am carrying."
"Do not be angry," said the second rogue, "but be careful. These woods are haunted."

The Carpenter's Carpet

The old man was a little worried now, but carried the goat further and he was met by the third rogue. "Good evening, sir," said the third rogue, "why are you carrying that donkey on your shoulders through these haunted woods?"

The old man was horrified. "Here, you take it!" he cried, thinking "it must be goblin with four legs, and not a goat!" He threw the goat down, and ran home as fast as he could, terrified. By trickery the three rogues got the old man's goat, and the poor old man lost his gold.

It is not always right to believe what other people tell you: there are still rogues in the woods.

.Diamond Cut Diamond

ONCE UPON A TIME there was man — a merchant — who
went to a far away land. There he worked hard, carefully
saving the money he earned, and after twelve years he had
quite a large amount of money. Now this was long before
we had banks to keep money in, and long before we could
send money safely from country to country. So Ahmed —
that was the merchant's name — wondered how he could
carry all his money back home, without its being stolen.
And he thought of a plan.

With his money Ahmed bought some magnificent jewels —
diamonds and rubies and emeralds — and locked them into
a little box which he kept under his robe — this was much
easier to carry than all the gold. And Ahmed bought some
very ordinary clothes, so that he looked like a poor man and
would not attract the attention of robbers.

Ahmed was able to walk quickly and safely along the roads
towards his home, and eventually he came to a city that was
only a few days' walk from his home. He decided that now
that he was nearly home, and he was not afraid of thieves
any more, he could buy better clothes, and return home
looking more like the rich man he really was. So he went to
the local market to see what he could buy.

There was one shop in the market that sold better silks,
more beautiful carpets, and more elegant clothes than all the
rest, and Ahmed went there to buy his new clothes. The
owner of this shop — his name was Beeka Mull — was
sitting, smoking his long silver pipe. Ahmed greeted him

25

politely, and began to buy things. Now Beeka Mull was a very shrewd man, and he soon felt sure that Ahmed was richer than he seemed to be. Beeka Mull invited Ahmed to eat lunch with him, and as they sat eating together, Beeka Mull asked Ahmed where he was going. Ahmed told him the name of his home village.

"Ah," said Beeka Mull, "you must be careful – there are many thieves on that road."
"Oh dear," though Ahmed, "I don't want to lose all my money when I am so near to home. What can I do with my box of jewels?" So Ahmed said to Beeka Mull "Sir, would you do me a favour? I have a small box that I would like to leave here. Could you lock it safely away for me and I will come back in a few days time with six strong men from my village to protect me, and claim it from you."
"I am sorry," said Beeka Mull, "I don't do that sort of business — I'm really not the right person to ask."
"Please," said Ahmed, "I don't know anyone else in this town — you must have some place where you keep your own precious things. Please look after this box for me."

Beeka Mull continued to refuse, and Ahmed continued to persuade him. At last Beeka Mull said he would look after Ahmed's box. Beeka Mull took Ahmed's little box of jewels and locked it in a large, strong chest with many other precious stones, and Ahmed thanked him, and left his shop to walk home.

In an Eastern bazaar all the shops are open, and all the other merchants could see that Ahmed and Beeka Mull were having a long talk to each other. Now — and I know this sounds horrid — most of the other merchants were thieves, and Beeka Mull was the worst of them. From time to time

Ahmed would stop at another shop and ask about Beeka Mull. Each of the other shopkeepers thought perhaps they would get something from what Beeka Mull was stealing, so each of these scoundrels lied and said "Oh yes, Beeka Mull is an honest and an honourable man."

So the merchant felt happy, and returned home. Within a week he came back to the city with six strong young men — nephews and friends — to protect him as he carried the box back home. Ahmed told his friends to wait in the centre of the city, and Ahmed went to the bazaar to fetch his box.

But Beeka Mull pretended not to know him. Ahmed said "Please Sir, may I have my box back, that you are looking after?"
"What box?" snapped Beeka Mull, "I don't look after other people's treasures. Be off with you!"
"But surely you remember me?" said Ahmed.
"Be off with you! Worthless beggar!" shouted Beeka Mull, "and get out of my shop!"

Well, several of the other stallholders came to help Beeka Mull, and they picked Ahmed up and flung him into the street. Ouch! Poor Ahmed! He was all bruised and scraped. He crawled off and curled up next to a nearby wall feeling very hurt, and miserable that he had lost all his money.

And there he sat for all the rest of the day. When evening time came, and the bazaar had closed for the day, Ahmed's friends shrugged their shoulders and said "Ahmed must have gone home by himself — let's go." So they went home too. And Ahmed still sat miserably by the wall.

When night time came there was a jolly fellow, a rich young man called Kooshy Ram, walking along the road of the

27

bazaar with a friend.

"Ah — a thief," said the friend.

"No," said Kooshy Ram, "thieves do not sit in full view like that. He looks miserable." Kooshy Ram asked Ahmed why he was sitting there, and Ahmed told him the full story.

"Oh Sir," said Ahmed, "there is nothing I can do to get back all my money."

"Nonsense!" exclaimed Kooshy Ram, "Even though Beeka Mull is the greatest thief in the whole bazaar, we will get your box back for you. Now come back with me and have dinner."

The next day, Kooshy Ram told Ahmed to go back and sit down near Beeka Mull's shop. "When you receive a signal," said Kooshy Ram, "I want you to go up to Beeka Mull and ask him politely for your box, and you will receive it." "How can I?" said Ahmed, "I have tried that and been refused." "Trust me," said Kooshy Ram, "and do exactly as I say."

So Ahmed sat down opposite Beeka Mull's shop all morning, and nothing happened. Early in the afternoon there was a stir at the far end of the bazaar — someone important or rich was coming, that was clear. And — yes — it was a palanquin being carried by four strong men. What's a palanquin? It is a chair that can be carried, and it is hidden behind silk curtains. And this palanquin looked wonderful, and the four strong men carrying it were richly dressed, and beside the palanquin walked another richly dressed man, followed by a servant, who was carrying a box.

The palanquin stopped outside Beeka Mull's shop. Beeka Mull was delighted that someone so rich was coming to do business with him. "What may I do for you good people?" said Beeka Mull, most politely.

The richly dressed man explained to Beeka Mull that in the palanquin was a relative of his — a lady — who was travelling. Because her husband was delayed, she could not travel on — would Beeka Mull be so kind as to look after a box of jewels for her? The servant brought forward the box, which was opened and Beeka Mull was astonished at the number of beautiful jewels in it. Beeka Mull's mouth watered — maybe he would be able to keep this box as he had kept Ahmed's much smaller box.

Just then Ahmed saw a hand come out of the palanquin, on the side away from the shop, and beckon him. Ahmed hesitated — the hand beckoned again. So Ahmed walked over to the shop and asked, "Please sir, may I have back the box of mine which you have on trust?"
Beeka Mull frowned, thinking that if Ahmed started to make a fuss again, then he might loose these new and richer customers — and the new box of jewels was so much larger than Ahmed's. "Certainly," said Beeka Mull, with a false smile, "I shall just go and get it."
And he went and got the little box and handed it to Ahmed, who unlocked it, and saw that all his treasures were there. Ahmed danced with joy in the road, screaming with laughter.

Just then a messenger ran up and saluted the palanquin. "The lady's husband has returned," said the messenger, all out of breath, "so there is no need to leave the jewels." Quickly the box was snapped shut and locked, and handed back to the servant.

29

The Carpenter's Carpet

Then there came a yell of laughter from inside the palanquin — and out of it stepped not a lady, but Kooshy Ram, who joined Ahmed dancing in the road and laughing. Beeka Mull stared at them for a moment, then he too flung off his turban, and joined them dancing and laughing in the street.

"Why are you dancing?" asked the messenger, "Ahmed the merchant is dancing because he has recovered all his money; Kooshy Ram is dancing because he has tricked you; but why are *you* dancing?"
"I am dancing," panted Beeka Mull, "because I knew thirteen different ways of deceiving people — but here is a fourteenth! That is why I dance!"

.Sweet Water

THERE WAS A MAN who lived with his family in a wilderness. They moved from place to place finding food for their camels and goats, but always came back to the same spring of water to drink. The water was bitter and salty, and they had never tasted any other.

One year there was a drought, the spring of water nearly dried up and was more salty than ever, and they could not find enough to feed their animals. So they had to move to another part of the desert, and they were in hardship. The man thought that perhaps the Calif — the king of that area — would be able to help them, so he took one camel to ride, and set off towards the city — the king's city he had heard of, but never seen.

On his way he found a pool of water, stagnant and muddy, and the mud had absorbed the salt. When the man tasted the water he was astonished — he did not know that sweet water existed — and he exclaimed "By all that is Great, this is the water of Paradise that has been sent for my aid. I shall take some of this to the king and he will surely listen to my plea to help my family." So he filled a goatskin bag with the water, and carried on his journey.

Now it happened that on that day the Calif, with his court, was out hunting, and they were in that region. When they saw the man they called "Where are you from?"
"From the desert."
"Where are you going?"
"To the court of the Calif."

31

The Carpenter's Carpet

"What gift are you bringing?"
"Water of Paradise."

The Calif said "Let me taste it."

When he was given the waterskin, the king indicated that it should be poured into bottles, and a small glass of the water was brought to him. As soon as the king had tasted the muddy water he realised what had happened. "You tell no lies," said the Calif. "What are you asking from me?"

And the man told how he and his family had been driven from their usual home by drought, and did not know how to find help except by begging at the Calif's feet. "Your request is granted," said the king, "on condition that you at once turn back and go no further." To this the man immediately agreed. The Calif ordered the waterskin to be filled with gold, and he sent a soldier to accompany the man back to his family.

When the man had gone the courtiers asked the king why he had acted as he did — it was only muddy water, and not very good water. "I told him to turn back immediately," said the Calif, because if he had continued on the way he was going, he would have come to the river, and then he would have thought his gift was worthless. And no-one who in honesty brings a worthy gift should leave my presence and feel in shame."

.*The Kurd's Camel*

ONCE UPON SOME TIME OR OTHER — I cannot tell you when, but I'm sure it was before last Wednesday — there was a man who had no money and was thrown in to prison for debt. But even while he was in prison he used to steal food from the other prisoners. He got quite fat, and the other prisoners were very cross. At last the other prisoners complained to the Cadi — he was the important man who looked after the prison.

The Cadi listened to what they said, and he called the penniless man. "Get out of this prison," ordered the Cadi, "and go back to your home." And the Cadi ordered that the man should be paraded in front of all the markets in the town, and along all the streets, and in the centre of every square in town where people meet.

Passing outside the prison there was a Kurd with a camel — he was returning to get some more firewood, which he sold. So one of the soldiers of the Cadi took this camel, and sat the fat prisoner on its back. The Kurd was not happy with this, as they did not give him any payment for the use of his camel. But the fat man was paraded through town, with loud criers proclaiming "This man is bankrupt. He owns nothing. Lend him nothing. If you complain about him, the Cadi will not listen. You have been warned: this man is bankrupt." And the Kurd followed along behind the little procession, complaining about not being paid for his camel.

At the end of the day, they let the fat man get off the camel. The Kurd came to him and said "My home is the other side

33

The Carpenter's Carpet

of town, and you have sat on my camel all day. I will let you off the price of the firewood I could have sold, but at least give me the price of the straw."

"Have you not been listening?" the fat bankrupt replied, "They have been shouting all day about me, telling everyone I have nothing, I have no money — but you seem not to have heard it! Simple greed must have filled your ears — so it is true that greed makes people deaf — and blind!"

.Think Ahead

A MAN WENT TO A GOLDSMITH. "Please let me have some scales," he said, "I want to weigh some gold."
"Go away," said the goldsmith, "I do not have a sieve."
"Give me the scales," said the man, "and don't make such silly jokes."
"I do not have a broom in the shop," said the goldsmith.
"Enough! Enough!" said the man, "stop pretending you are deaf or stupid, and just let me have the scales!"

"I heard what you said," said the goldsmith, "I am not deaf, and I am not stupid. But your hands shake, and the gold you want to weigh consists of tiny shavings. So fragments of your gold will spill. Then you will ask for a broom so you can search for your gold in the dust. Then you will ask for a sieve to separate the gold from the dust. I saw the end from the beginning. Before you start anything, think where it may end."

Fringes of the Carpet

THE STORIES in "The Carpenter's Carpet" are teaching stories from old traditions and religions. The three Krishna stories about God's hidden power & personal contact ("Birthday Party", "A Pot of Butter" and "Swimming") come from Hinduism. From "The 1001 Arabian Nights" and its Islamic background, we have "The Woodcutter's Horse", "The Carpenter's Carpet" — remember to ask for the opposite of what the other carpet would give you — and "Think Ahead". The Sufi teaching tales from The Masnavi ("The Kurd's Camel" and "Sweet Water") show how the mind can move faster than all things but be deflected by inattention, and that the heart is strongest of all. "The Old Man and the Goat" and "Dreamer's Well" come from The Panchatantra. The story of "Noah" is from the Old Testament, and "Yellow Coat" and "Sparrows" are from the Apocryphal New Testament. "Diamond Cut Diamond" is a Sikh tale from Bengal.

Pay attention and dream; think far and look near; remember that love is the most powerful weapon of all. Smile — and perhaps you will find another Woodcutter's way of moving between worlds.

www.ingramcontent.com/pod-product-compliance
Lightning Source LLC
Chambersburg PA
CBHW071352130626
46556CB00005B/2148